SUPER HAPPY MAGIC FOREST
AND THE DISTANT DESERT
LONG
OXFORD
UNIVERSITY PRESS

THE SUPER HAPPY HEROES

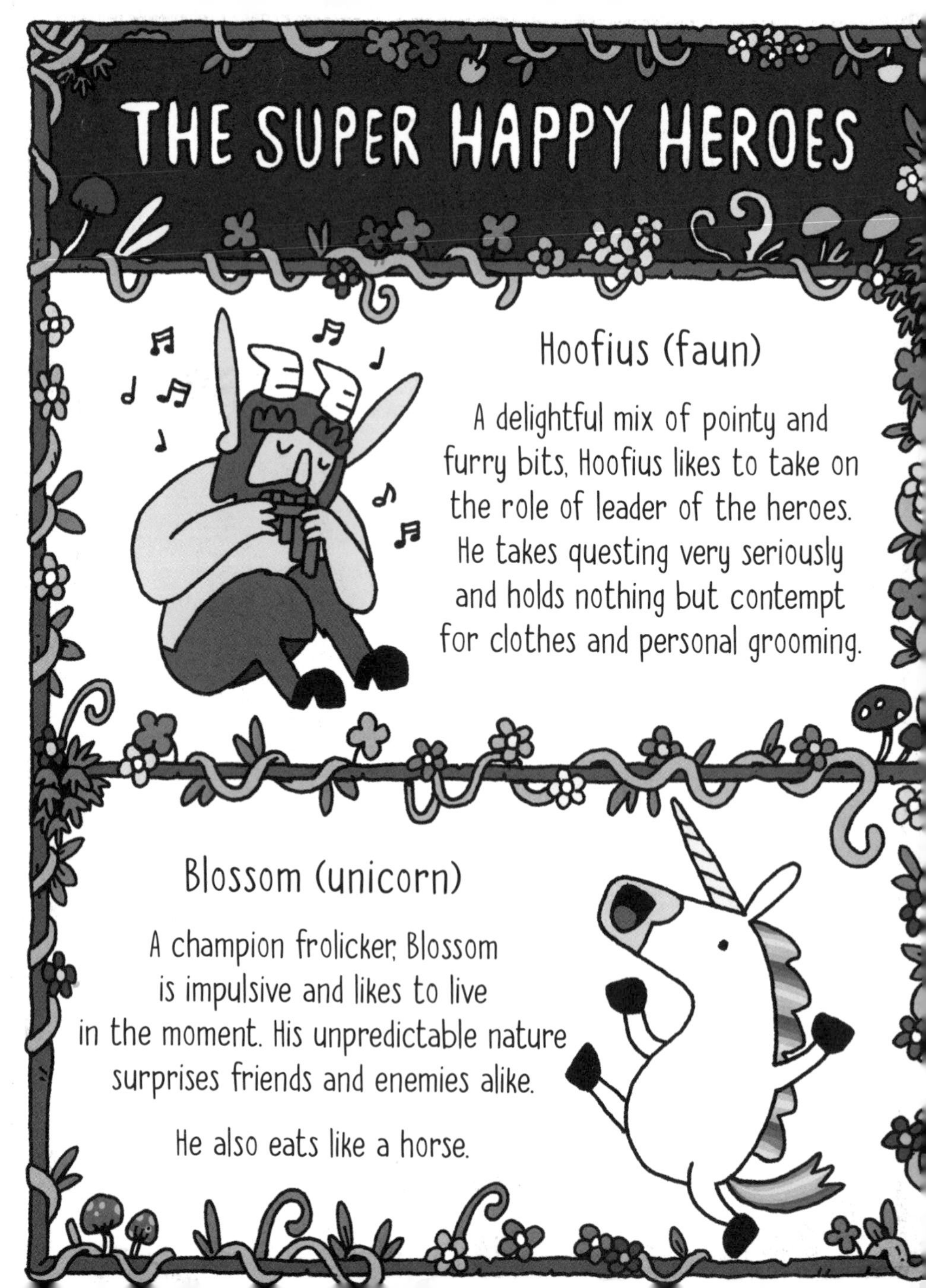

Hoofius (faun)

A delightful mix of pointy and furry bits, Hoofius likes to take on the role of leader of the heroes. He takes questing very seriously and holds nothing but contempt for clothes and personal grooming.

Blossom (unicorn)

A champion frolicker, Blossom is impulsive and likes to live in the moment. His unpredictable nature surprises friends and enemies alike.

He also eats like a horse.

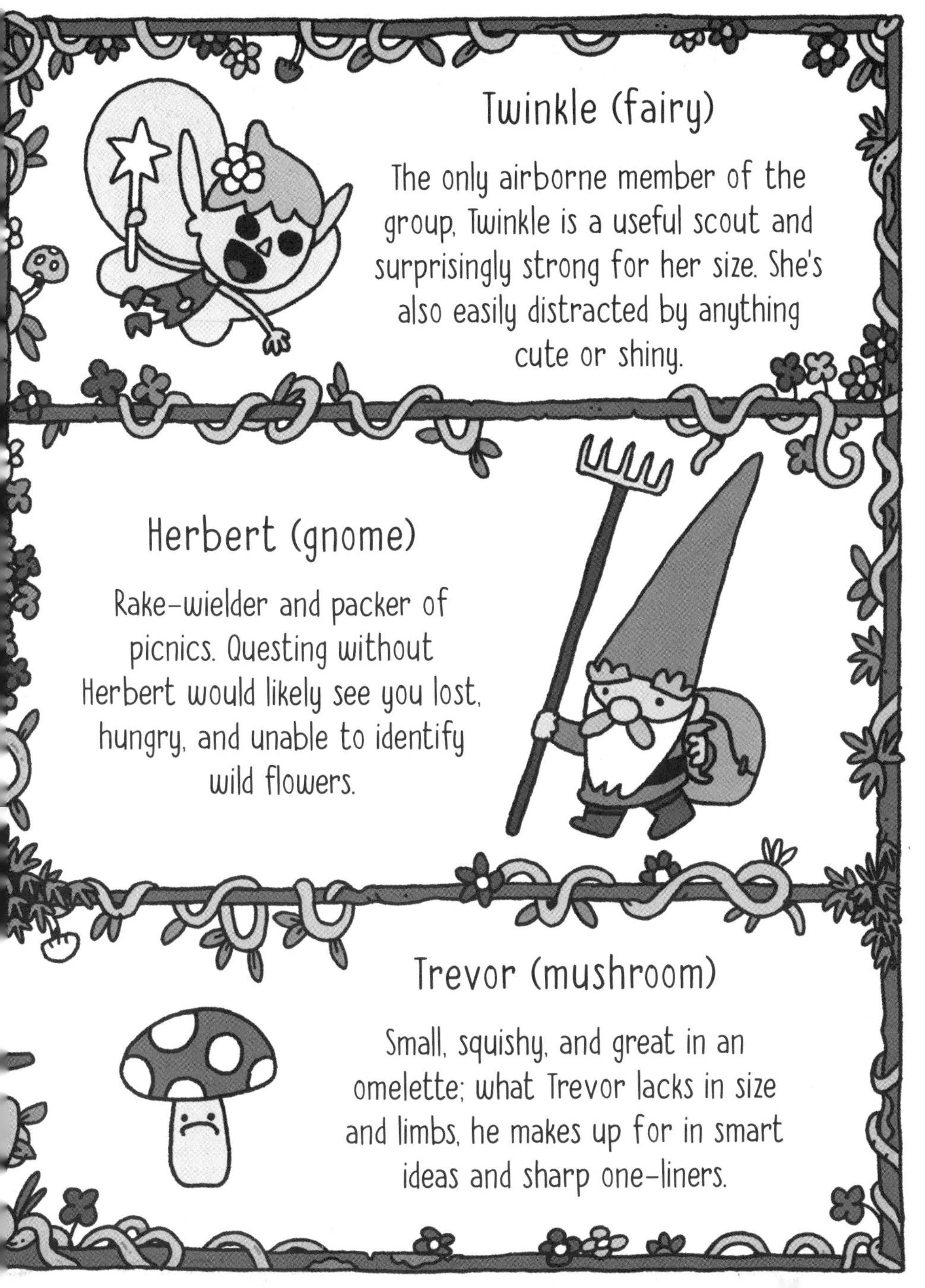

Twinkle (fairy)

The only airborne member of the group, Twinkle is a useful scout and surprisingly strong for her size. She's also easily distracted by anything cute or shiny.

Herbert (gnome)

Rake-wielder and packer of picnics. Questing without Herbert would likely see you lost, hungry, and unable to identify wild flowers.

Trevor (mushroom)

Small, squishy, and great in an omelette; what Trevor lacks in size and limbs, he makes up for in smart ideas and sharp one-liners.

CHAPTER ONE

OPENING NIGHT JITTERS

You might say that it was an evening like any other in the Super Happy Magic Forest. But you'd be wrong. All sorts of characters from gnomes and pixies to flowers with big, huge faces gathered inside a large tent, sipping on the finest boxed fruit drinks, and enjoying the tastiest nibbles around. This was the cultural highlight of the year.

It was the grand opening of . . .

The Gnome Tashwhisker exhibition!
What's a Gnome Tashwhiskey?
Gnome TashWHISKER was the greatest gnome explorer ever! Probably.
PRESS
Come one, come all to the greatest collection of old junk you've ever seen!

CAREFULLY ARRANGED OLD STUFF
Refreshment for you, sir?
DANGER! ANCIENT RELIC. DO NOT TOUCH!
Too many canapés.

Herbert the gnome had found boxes of his great-great-grandfather's travel journals and souvenirs tucked away in his attic. So he'd gladly taken on the task of creating an exhibition of the many wonders that Gnome Tashwhisker had discovered.

For this fine occasion, he was joined by his friends Hoofius the faun, Twinkle the fairy, Blossom the unicorn, and Trevor the mushroom. The five friends were commonly known as the heroes throughout the Super Happy Magic Forest because they loved going on epic quests.

It's more because nobody else can be bothered to go.

They had all helped Herbert arrange the collection of relics, diaries, and doodads. It offered everybody a glimpse into the wonders of a world beyond the lollipop ponds and candyfloss caves of the Super Happy Magic Forest. And for Herbert, this was a chance to share the remarkable life of his ancestor.

Opening night was shaping up to be a storming success. Everyone loved the unusual artefacts on display.

Things were going so well that Tiddlywink the pixie couldn't resist being the centre of attention. As a member of the Council of Happiness, he knew that events like this were a perfect opportunity to boost his popularity, and if everyone went away thinking that HE was to thank for such a wonderful time then even better. He stood on a stool and tapped a spoon on his glass to get the crowd's attention.

Ladies, gentlemen, plant-folk, and mythical beasts of all kinds! Who will join me in a toast?

The guests stopped for a moment and got ready to raise their glasses to Herbert and the heroes.

'Yes, indeed!' continued Tiddlywink. 'A toast to those who made tonight possible. That's right—your friends on the Council of Happiness!'

There were groans and the odd bit of applause, as the pixie beamed from ear to ear and raised his glass higher. The other three members of the council—Butterfly Horse, Sunshine, and Admin Bunny—looked more than a tad embarrassed at him taking the credit.

I suppose there was a bit of paperwork involved . . .

'Typical Tiddlywink!' whispered Herbert to his friends. 'Taking all the credit for our hard work.'

The pixie launched into a self-congratulatory speech so long and boring that Blossom couldn't help but become distracted by a nearby relic.

It was an odd cube split into squares. They were set in rows on every side, with strange little pictures on them. Every row and side of the cube matched. Blossom twisted and turned it this way and that—which was no easy thing when you had hooves.

The air around him seemed to darken with every twist. Eventually Blossom plonked the cube back down and moved on. Even for a unicorn, he didn't have the longest attention span. He continued to nose and prod at this and that while everyone else's attention was on Tiddlywink.

But soon enough, murmurs of discontent rippled through the crowd and quickly turned to cries of alarm. It was more than Tiddlywink could take. He jumped down and barged his way through to demand answers for the commotion.

The cube. Tiddlywink frowned and picked it up. Big mistake.

Phew! It didn't blow after all.

Panic gripped the tent as their fourth favourite councillor was sucked into the cube. Herbert and the other heroes pushed through to get a closer look.

'Oh no. Oh no, oh no!' stammered Herbert at the sight of the cube with all the sides jumbled up.

One-star reviews in the *Pixie Village Gazette* were the least of his worries now.

Tiddlywink had disappeared.

CHAPTER TWO

PEAKY BLUNDERS

If you had told some sections of the Super Happy Magic Forest that Tiddlywink the pixie had gone, you might have heard the odd bottle popping at the news. But not like this. This was serious. And Blossom knew it. Something heavy dropped within him to the pit of his belly. And it had nothing to do with the toffee apples he was eating.

Herbert grasped the cube and twisted the sides in a panic. 'Someone must have tampered with it!' spluttered the gnome. 'I left signs saying not to touch. Did anyone see who did this?'

Blossom froze. His friends all shook their heads. Blossom found his head shaking too. *Phew*, thought the unicorn. *Nobody saw me do it*. He didn't know exactly what had happened to the pixie, but it was bad.

'So, what is that thing? And why did it swallow up Tiddlywink?' asked Admin Bunny, afraid to get too close.

'It's a cursed cube,' said a bewildered-looking Herbert. 'When the pictures aren't the same on every side, it's a matter of time before it captures whoever is closest and traps them within. I must say that I'm flabbergasted it still works. This is an ancient device!'

I see. I'll file an accident report.
THIS WAS NO ACCIDENT! HERBERT IS TO BLAME!
WHOA! The cube can talk.

'IT'S NOT THE CUBE! IT'S ME, TIDDLYWINK!' spat the pixie. 'AND HERBERT HAS CAPTURED ME IN HIS PRISON OF DARKNESS!'

'It wasn't Herbert's fault!' blurted Blossom.

'Yeah! Someone must have tampered with it,' said Twinkle, defending her friend.

'WELL, WHEN I FIND OUT WHO DID, I'LL DO EVERYTHING IN MY POWER TO BOOT THEM OUT OF THE SUPER HAPPY MAGIC FOREST FOREVER!' ranted the pixie. The words wavered and seemed to echo. But Blossom heard them loud and clear.

'No need to worry. We'll have you out in a jiffy!' said Herbert. 'We just need to complete the puzzle and get all the pictures on the same side. How hard can it be?'

The sharpest minds in the forest all had a try.

Turn that bit left! Or maybe right!
...
No, no! Keep on twisting!
Rotate the top row anticlockwise!
Smash it open with a hammer!

It was no use.

'Let's face it . . . we are all too stupid to figure this out,' said Trevor.

'TELL ME SOMETHING I DON'T KNOW!' grumbled Tiddlywink.

Luckily, Herbert had been busy flicking through *Gnome Tashwhisker's Desert Diaries* and had stumbled upon a solution.

'It says here that in the Distant Desert there's an Almighty Oracle that knows everything there is to know about anything. We could go there and ask it how to solve the puzzle!'

'THEN WHAT ARE YOU WAITING FOR?' cried Tiddlywink. 'TO THE DESERT WITH YOU!'

And so, the heroes found themselves packing for another quest, this time to the Distant Desert.

Even Blossom perked up at the idea.

It was a long, long journey. And the desert felt even more distant with Tiddlywink in tow.

ARE WE THERE YET?
ARE WE THERE YET? ARE WE . . . HELLO?
Zzzz . . .

'DON'T THINK THIS IS OVER ONCE I'M OUT OF HERE,' moaned the pixie as early signs of the hot desert air started to blow past them. 'THIS DEATHTRAP OF YOURS SHOULD NEVER HAVE BEEN ON SHOW. YOUR DAYS OF LIVING IN THE SUPER HAPPY MAGIC FOREST ARE NUMBERED, HERBERT.'

'It wasn't his fault!' repeated Blossom.

'THEN WHO ELSE IS TO BLAME?' asked Tiddlywink. 'I WANT NAMES!'

Blossom couldn't bring himself to own up. It wasn't just the wrath of Tiddlywink he was afraid of. He had ruined Herbert's big night too. Blossom figured he'd be booted from the forest AND Herbert would never talk to him again if he said what had actually happened.

Nobody can know, thought Blossom. *Once we get Tiddlywink out of the box and back home it'll all be forgotten about*, he told himself.

The group, at last, arrived at what could only be the Distant Desert. A helpful sign showed a map of the area.

Gosh, it's a bit warm. I overdressed!

CREEPY CRYPT (IT'S ACTUALLY MORE OF A TOMB)
THE ALMIGHTY ORACLE (NOT TO SCALE)
CACTUS CANYON (HUG THE LOCALS AT YOUR OWN RISK)
CRYSTAL PEAK (A BREATHTAKING CLIMB FOR BREATHTAKING VIEWS)
YOU ARE HERE (IT'S NOT TOO LATE TO TURN BACK)

OASIS MINOR
(BEGGARS CAN'T BE CHOOSERS)
SEA OF SAND
('DUNES OF DEATH' WAS OFF-PUTTING TO TOURISTS)
OASIS MAJOR
(SIT DOWN, DRINK UP)

Herbert spotted the rocky peak upon which the Almighty Oracle floated. Even though Tiddlywink didn't have to trek up it in blistering heat, the pixie was still grumbling about something.

'HURRY UP, HEROES! I'M DUE TO OPEN A NEW RAINBOW SLIDE AT LAKE SPARKLE TOMORROW. WE CAN'T HAVE SUNSHINE CUTTING THE RIBBON INSTEAD OF ME. HE'LL DO IT ALL WRONG!'

The heroes huffed and puffed as they climbed up the cliffs. When they arrived at the top, they punched the air in delight. The Almighty Oracle was exactly where it should be.

But there was just one problem . . .

A stone sat beneath it, with three indents and the words 'INSERT TRIAL GEMS HERE'. Herbert frantically flicked through the *Desert Diaries*, all hot and very bothered by the change in circumstances.

'Oh dear,' he said at last, removing his hat and fanning himself with it. He read out the offending passage.

'Only adventurers who have completed the Desert Trials and have thus earned three trial gems are worthy of waking the Oracle.'

Always read the fine print.

CHAPTER THREE

WISHFUL THINKING

To say Tiddlywink took the news badly would be undercooking it. He practically hit the roof of his cube when he found out he wouldn't be home in time to cut the ribbon on the rainbow slide. Or maybe ever home at all.

Tiddlywink's outburst startled Blossom, and he stumbled backwards over an old boot that was lying in the dust. Curiously, smoke started to rise from inside. The way Blossom's luck was going, he wouldn't have been surprised if the boot burst into flames.

The smoke weaved its way into the air and began to take shape before his eyes. The other heroes gathered around nervously. Herbert had his rake ready just in case he needed to give whatever it was a bop.

Greetings, lowly mortals! I am the genie of the boot.

'Wow, a genie!' gasped Blossom, feeling his luck turn.

'That's right, Horsey!' came the reply. 'Bingo is my name-o. I am here to grant you THREE WISHES. So, let's be having you!'

A thousand thoughts rushed through Blossom's head all at once. The things he could do with three wishes . . .

'I wish for Tiddlywink to be freed from the cursed cube!' said Blossom. He still had two other wishes, after all.

'Your wish is my command!' said the genie. She cracked her fingers and began to limber up. 'Yep, just give me a second here . . .' she said, whirling her arms around like a windmill, '. . . just geeing myself up!'

At last, the moment arrived.

But nothing happened.

Where's Tiddlywink?
I'M STILL IN HERE! THAT GENIE IS A FRAUD!

'Err . . . that was just a practice run,' said Bingo. 'I'll get it this time. Just you watch!'

The heroes stood in the sweltering heat as Bingo . . . well, they weren't sure what Bingo was doing.

Your . . .
. . . wish . . .
. . . is my . . .
COMMAND!
Err . . .
Hgnhnf!
Poot

'Is this going to finish today?' Hoofius whispered to the others. But Bingo had run out of puff. And Tiddlywink was still stuck in a box.

Not going to lie, that was a bit of a let-down.

'Bingo, are you okay?' asked Blossom.

'I tried,' said the genie. 'But I can't. I can't grant wishes without my magic lamp!'

'YOU COULD HAVE TOLD US THAT BEFORE YOUR SONG-AND-DANCE ROUTINE!' the pixie complained. 'EVERY SECOND I'M

TRAPPED IN HERE, THE SUPER HAPPY MAGIC FOREST IS FALLING APART.'

The heroes could only wonder at the carefree fun that was following Tiddlywink's departure. It was a shame they weren't there to enjoy it themselves.

'Where is your lamp?' asked Twinkle.

Bingo saddened. 'I don't know. It was taken from me long ago.'

So, I have a genie that can't grant wishes?
Bingo.

'Do you remember where you last saw it?' asked Twinkle.

'Of course I do!' said Bingo. 'It was only a thousand years ago, back when I was the personal genie of the grand empress who ruled over this desert. The three wishes I granted helped her create the most amazing civilization the world had ever seen.

'But I got a bit caught up in all the fun and granted her a fourth wish by mistake.'

Rule one of the Genie Code: Genies can grant only three wishes to any one lamp-wielder.

'What's so bad about granting extra wishes?' asked Blossom.

'Granting more than three wishes to one person can have terrible consequences for the wisher,' explained Bingo. 'The wishes they made could unravel or backfire in unpredictable ways. After I granted the fourth wish, everything began to shake, and the civilization I helped create crumbled to the ground.

'I tried to pretend it wasn't my fault. But the empress seized my lamp and said I could never be allowed to grant wishes again. I was cast out and cursed to wander the desert as the centuries ticked by.'

It's okay. We've all done things that we regret.
Yup. I tried mint ice cream once.

'All I want is to grant wishes again,' said Bingo. 'That is my purpose!'

'BACK OF THE QUEUE,' said Tiddlywink from within the cube. 'WE'VE ALL GOT OUR PROBLEMS!'

'Maybe I could help,' said Bingo. 'I know all about the desert trials, but only mortals are allowed to take them. If I help you all to get your annoying friend out of the box, then maybe you could use one of your Oracle questions to ask where my lamp is?'

Not everyone was sure about letting an empire-ruining genie tag along, and her attempts at granting wishes had been a load of hot air in more ways than one.

But they'd need Bingo's help quicker than they realized.

Trevor was in trouble.

CHAPTER FOUR

ENCHANTED RUG

'Is the mushroom supposed to look like that?' asked Bingo, pointing to Trevor.

He was crispier and drier than any living mushroom had ever been before.

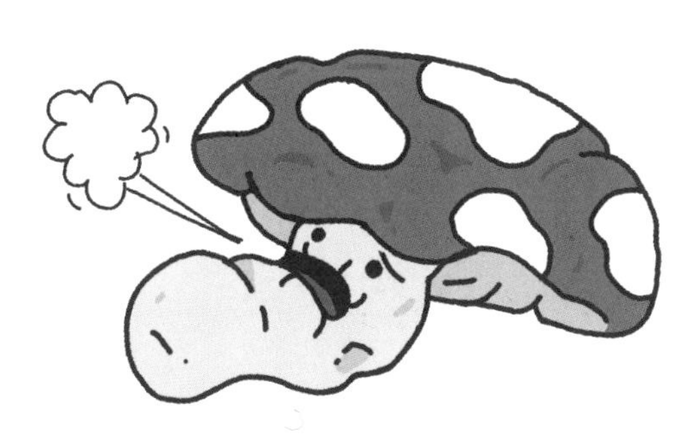

'Water! Quickly!' cried Hoofius. Herbert hurriedly took out his flask from his rucksack. But the few remaining drops of water evaporated into thin air as soon as he poured them out.

'We need oasis water!' cried Bingo. 'Quick, we'll take the genie blimp!'

Bingo may have lost all her magic powers, but she still had a trick or two up her sleeve. She breathed in so deep that she started inflating. Soon they were all floating through the desert heat to a blurry blue dot in the distance.

We're so high up . . . I don't think flying is really for me.
You would be a terrible fairy.

The oasis flickered into view, and the heroes could see exotic-looking trees and turquoise water that made Lake Sparkle seem like a swamp by comparison. Bingo breathed out, and they lowered through the palms and landed in soft sand. Blossom launched Trevor towards the water like a Frisbee.

Trevor soaked up the water like a sponge, and his eyes blinked open. Soon the other heroes were jumping in too, much to Tiddlywink's annoyance.

HERBERT? WHAT'S GOING ON? YOU'D BETTER NOT BE FROLICKING!

Bingo said Trevor's recovery was all down to oasis water having magical revitalizing properties. Herbert filled up his flask and a little travel-sized plant mister to keep his mushroom friend from drying out again.

This should keep you squishy!

The heroes now agreed that Bingo's knowledge of the desert would be invaluable on their quest for trial gems. And if they could help find her lamp in return, it seemed like everyone was a winner.

Blossom was happy to have Bingo along. Suddenly his own mistake didn't seem quite so bad. *Everyone deserves a chance to*

put things right, he thought. It felt like he and Bingo were on little quests of their own.

'Uh-oh,' mumbled Herbert as another problem arose.

The ice cream sandwiches have melted.

For all Herbert's smarts in bringing a plant mister to the desert, packing ice cream sandwiches wasn't the gnome's finest hour.

'We should have our picnic now,' he suggested. 'There might be nothing left to eat if we leave it much longer. And look! There's a picnic rug all ready and waiting.'

Stretched out in the sand was indeed a rug.

Herbert settled on it and started unpacking the wet and sticky picnic.

But the rug was having none of it.

The Super Happy heroes were used to picnicking in challenging conditions: on snowy mountains, in lava fields, during bee attacks, you name it. But the picnic rug had never revolted before.

'Bingo, what's going on?' asked Hoofius.

'Magic carpet,' replied Bingo. 'They come to the oasis to rest in the shade. That's a feisty one!'

It wasn't long before Herbert was heaved off and his head was buried in the sand.

'If you stay on long enough, it will accept you as its rider,' said Bingo. 'I reckon it would be a pretty handy way for you mortals to get around. You all have slow legs or no legs at all.'

Blossom was already creeping up on the carpet as Herbert shook the sand from his beard.

The race to wrangle a magic carpet was on.

No surprises here.
Wait!
Can't . . . breathe!
Hey! I think I've got it!

In the end, the hours Twinkle had spent riding Blossom as he frolicked through the meadows of the Super Happy Magic Forest were enough to seal the deal. The fairy held on until the carpet calmed down—but it still seemed to wriggle whenever Herbert tried to lay out the picnic on it.

'I think it operates a no food or drink policy,' said Bingo, pointing to the care instructions on the label.

Magic carpet made from 100% magic and wool. Keep away from food, drinks, and fire. Hand-wash only.

'Oh, sorry,' said Herbert, giving the carpet an apologetic stroke.

The heroes ate what they could away from the carpet, to the sounds of Tiddlywink, who seemed to be operating his usual no patience or politeness policy.

CAN WE GET A MOVE ON? ADMIN BUNNY WILL TAKE MY OFFICE IF IT'S LEFT UNGUARDED FOR MUCH LONGER. SHE HAS ALWAYS WANTED IT. IT HAS A SOUTH-FACING WINDOW!

But soon enough, they were all soaring through the skies.
It's like a WHOLE NEW WORLD!
Careful what you say.
The first trial was soon to begin.

CHAPTER FIVE

PRICKLY CUSTOMERS

'Magic Carpet, take us to Cactus Canyon please!' ordered Bingo, remembering her manners. You wouldn't want to upset the carpet when it was *this* high up.

Down below, the scene of their first trial unfolded before them. It looked like some kind of obstacle course . . .
BAYING MOB
FUN SLIDES
CLIMBING WALL
START

FINISH
THE FINAL CLIMB
DUELLING PLATFORMS
THE DRINK
SPINNING CACTUS TOWERS

The carpet skimmed across the sand and settled to let them off. The canyon was eerily quiet, and there were cacti as far as the eye could see. The heroes felt that they weren't alone.

All around them, the cacti twitched to life and shuffled towards them.

'These lowly mortals are here to attempt your trial!' announced Bingo.

'DID YOU HEAR THAT, FOLKS?' came a loud voice that boomed off the canyon walls.

WE HAVE OURSELVES SOME CHALLENGERRRRRS!

The cacti burst into a frenzy of excitement, and they began to jostle for the best position to watch the action as the rules were read out.

'TO WIN A TRIAL GEM, AT LEAST ONE CHALLENGER MUST MAKE IT TO THE END OF THE COURSE . . .'

'That seems fine,' said Hoofius to the others, fancying their chances.

But the commentator wasn't finished.

'. . . AND THEY WILL BE UP AGAINST . . . **THE GUARDIAAAANNNNNS!**'

'There's always a catch,' said Trevor.

The cheers turned raucous, as four big and fierce cacti folk appeared. They were introduced one by one.

'PRICKLE RICK!
PR
NEEDLE NED!
NN
THE OUCHIE TWINS!
AND OF COURSE . . .
STINGIN' SALLY!'
SS

'Oh wow, I've always wanted to see Stingin' Sally in action!' said Bingo, getting caught up in the excitement. The heroes frowned at her. 'I mean—you can do it, mortals!' she said, giving them an apologetic thumbs up.

The heroes took their places at the starting line as Bingo sat herself among the feverish crowd. Above the noise, Tiddlywink piped up from within the cube.

'REMEMBER, HEROES. FORGET EVERYTHING YOU HEARD ABOUT IT BEING THE TAKING PART THAT COUNTS. FAILURE IS NOT AN OPTION!'

'He is the worst cheerleader ever,' said Trevor, as the starting horn sounded.

'THEY'RE OFF! AND ALREADY THE GNOME IS HAVING TROUBLE WITH THE CLIMBING WALL!'
Herbert's many talents did not include climbing, and the challenge was made more difficult with Tiddlywink's own brand of coaching.
YOU'RE USELESS! YOU SHOULD HAVE STRAPPED ME TO THE UNICORN!

'Here comes Prickle Rick!' roared the commentator. The crowd cheered as the guardian began climbing the wall at an expert pace. He was hunting down the heroes.

'LOOKS LIKE THERE'S GNOME PLACE TO HIDE FOR THIS CHALLENGER!'

Herbert was helpless.

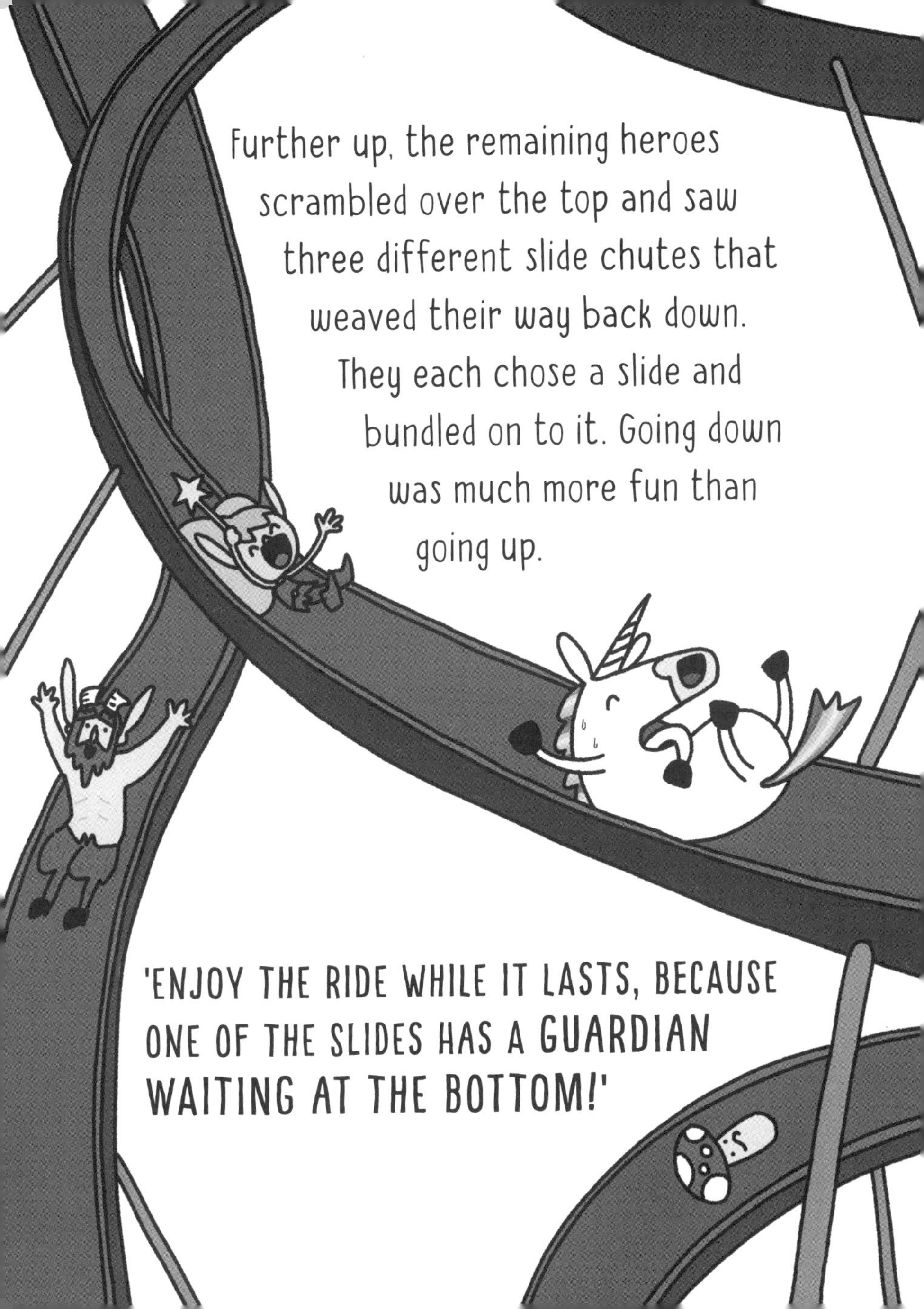

Further up, the remaining heroes scrambled over the top and saw three different slide chutes that weaved their way back down. They each chose a slide and bundled on to it. Going down was much more fun than going up.

'ENJOY THE RIDE WHILE IT LASTS, BECAUSE ONE OF THE SLIDES HAS A **GUARDIAN** WAITING AT THE BOTTOM!'

The chutes spat the heroes out into the sand before they had a chance to think.

Needle Ned was waiting for Hoofius.

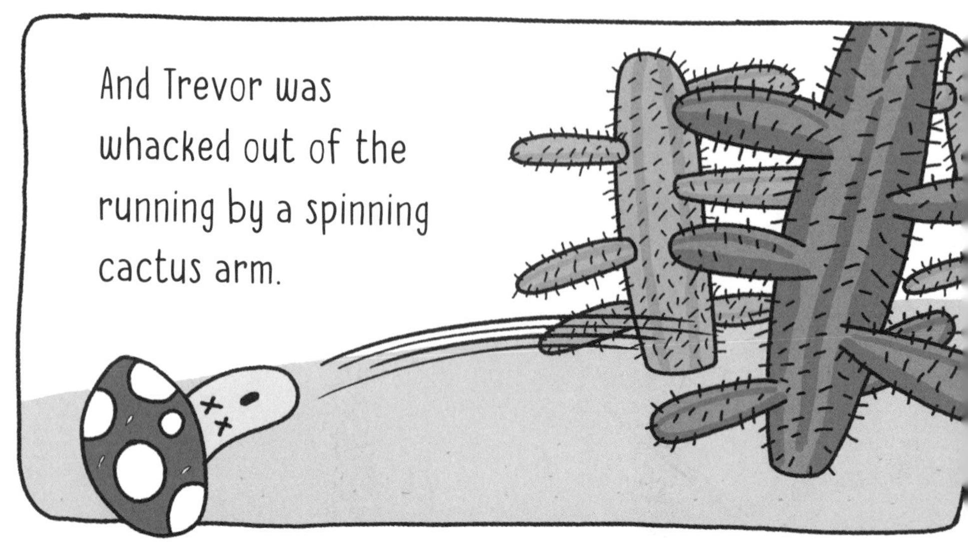

And Trevor was whacked out of the running by a spinning cactus arm.

'THAT'S THREE DOWN, TWO TO GO!' The crowd was going wild. **'BUT CAN THEY SURVIVE . . . THE DUELLING PLATFORMS?'**

Blossom had picked up a duelling club and was frantically bopping at the Ouchie Twins who stood on the opposite platform.

The combatants whacked and parried blow after blow. The unicorn was tiring.

'Blossom! Tag team!' urged Twinkle. Blossom hopped off the platform, and Twinkle took over with a fresh pair of arms. The crowd cheered. Even the twins were impressed.

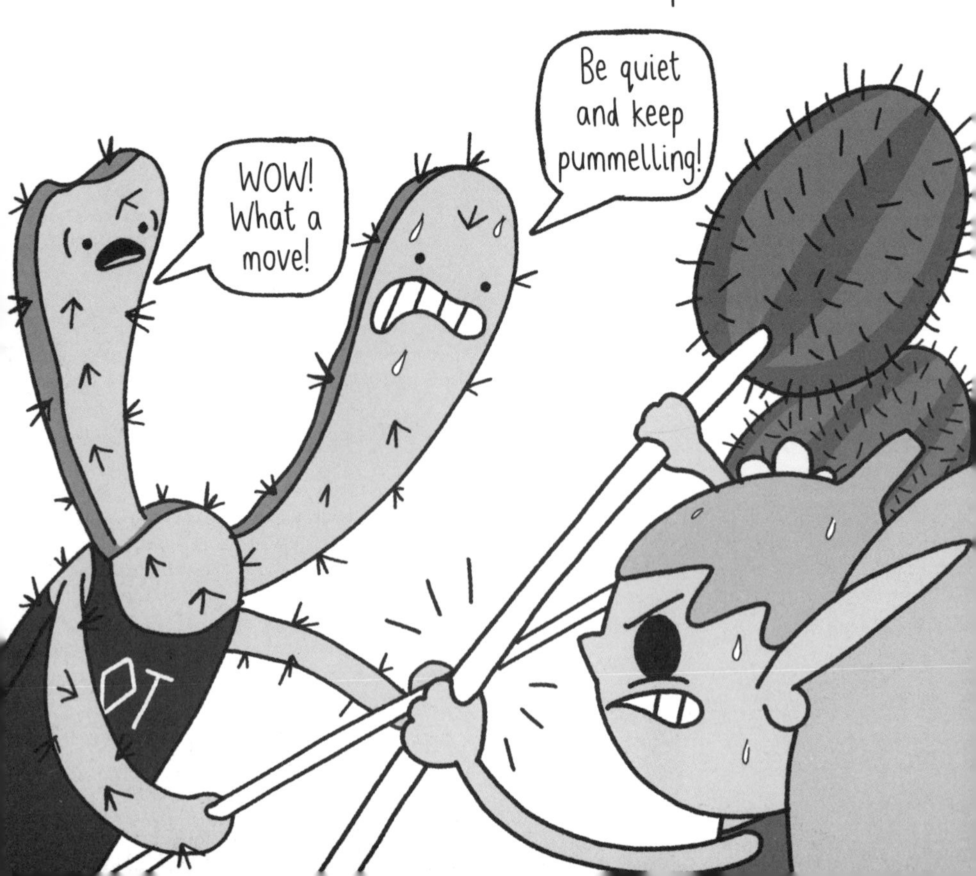

Twinkle was more than used to giving folks little lifts through their forest home. You might say it gave her arms a certain degree of strength that you wouldn't expect from a fairy. It was too much for the guardians.

'AND THE OUCHIE TWINS ARE IN THE DRINK!' squealed the commentator as the twins splashed down from the platform. The crowd booed at seeing their guardians bested by a challenger. Twinkle threw down the club and faced the rows of spectators.

Blossom grabbed the fairy and pulled her across the platforms to the final stage: a slope with the trial gem gleaming at the top.

Is this it?
Looks like they ran out of ideas.

All they had to do was climb up and take it.

CHAPTER SIX

GAME OVER

'What are we waiting for? Let's go!' cried Blossom, bounding up the slope. This was his chance to secure the first gem. If the others ever did find out he was responsible for trapping Tiddlywink in the cube, then at least he could say he did everything he could to get him out.

I'll save you, Tiddlywink!

'IT ALL COMES DOWN TO THIS! CAN THE CHALLENGERS GET PAST THE CROWD FAVOURITE . . . **STINGIN' SALLY?'**

Blossom was halfway up when the last guardian appeared at the top. Stingin' Sally began flexing to the cheers of the crowd, who began to chant, 'DROP THE BALLS! DROP THE BALLS! DROP THE BALLS!'

Sally tugged a lever and tipped a cascade of cactus balls down the slope.

Blossom was swept away.

'OOOF! IS THE UNICORN DONE FOR?'
The commentator could barely be heard above the feverish noise.

Twinkle rushed to her friend and dug him out from the pile of cactus balls, getting more than a few needle stings along the way.

Blossom, are you okay?
I think I swallowed one. Or maybe ten.

There was no way Blossom could continue, and every chance he'd be doing prickly poops for days to come.

'We need to give her a taste of her own medicine!' said Twinkle. 'Blossom, remember the time you swallowed that fiery gumball and we had to squeeze you until it shot back up?'

Blossom would never forget. The gumball set his stomach on fire, and it smashed a gnome's window it came back up so fast. He nodded and just about managed to get back on his hooves.

'It's time for the unicorn cannon!' cheered Twinkle.

Stingin' Sally was parading around at the top of the slope. She never expected the cactus balls to start coming back up.

But that's what they did.

The guardian turned around and took one on the chin. She lost her footing and went rolling down the slope. The crowd gasped. This was not in the script.

Twinkle fluttered up to the unguarded trial gem.

'THE CHALLENGERS HAVE DONE IT! THEY'VE BEATEN THE GUARDIANS AND CLAIMED THE TRIAL GEM! WHAT INCREDIBLE SCENES WE'VE WITNESSED HERE TODAY. TO CELEBRATE, THERE IS NOW FIFTY PER CENT OFF ALL ITEMS IN THE SOUVENIR SHOP!'

The commentator's words were met with deafening cheers as cactus folk shuffled to the shop for the epic savings. It seemed the heroes were the new crowd favourites. Bingo was first on the scene.

Twinkle's friends caught up to her, some a bit more groggily than others. It had been a brutal bout of exercise.

'I still enjoyed it more than the mushroom fun run we do every year,' said Trevor.

'They sure put on a show,' said Bingo. 'That was some top-notch entertainment. And you got the gem! Hey, what's the matter? Let's see some HYPE!'

The heroes were mostly lying around moaning and pinching prickles out of themselves. Herbert gave everyone a blast of the mister. The oasis water helped soothe all their bumps and bruises.

'GOOD WORK, HEROES!' chimed Tiddlywink. 'NOW LET'S GO ASK THAT ORACLE TO GET ME OUT OF HERE.'

The heroes all looked at each other.

'Awk-waaaarrrd!' said Bingo, grimacing.

'Um, we still need two more gems, Tiddlywink,' Hoofius said hesitantly. 'We need three in total.'

A silence followed as Tiddlywink came to terms with the full extent of the quest.

And then came the meltdown.

'YOU MEAN I HAVE TO SIT IN HERE LIKE A LEMON WHILE YOU FIVE AND THAT GLORIFIED CLOUD OF YOURS TRY TO LUCK YOUR WAY TO *TWO* MORE GEMS?'

'Not like a lemon,' said Blossom thoughtfully. 'More like an egg. An egg in a box.'

'You always know the right thing to say, Blossom,' said Trevor. Bingo ushered them away from the cube, leaving Tiddlywink to rant to himself while they enjoyed a bit of peace before the next trial.

I'LL GIVE YOU EGG IN A BOX! WISH I'D NEVER GONE TO THAT SILLY EXHIBITION! YOU CAN KISS GOODBYE TO ANY FUTURE COUNCIL FUNDING, HERBERT! HERBERT? HERBERT? COME BACK! PLEASE . . .

'Don't worry, friends, I think the next trial is less painful,' said Bingo. 'It's more to do with smarts. Brains. That sort of thing.'

Blossom groaned at the thought.

Once everyone was ready, they picked up the cursed cube and boarded the carpet.

'To the Creepy Crypt, please!' called Bingo.

The carpet whooshed into the air towards their next trial.

'Aren't crypts full of gross things like bones and skulls?' asked Twinkle.

'Yup,' said Bingo. 'Gotta store mortals somewhere once they bite the dust.'

Soon they touched down on to the sand.

The second trial lay within the darkness ahead.
CRE PY CRYP
Any tips for this trial, Bingo?
Nope. Most go in but don't live to tell the tale.
Can we just do the cactus one again?

CHAPTER SEVEN

BURNING QUESTIONS

The trial got off to a rough start when Bingo noticed a sign after they landed the carpet.

Oh great! We have to pay for carpet parking.
HAVE YOU PAID?
P

The heroes approached the entrance as the genie fumbled in her pockets for loose change. A voice echoed out from within.

'ONLY ONE CONTESTANT AT A TIME. HOOFIUS—COME ON DOWN!'

'How does it . . . know my name?' trembled Hoofius, treading carefully down some steps into the darkness and out of sight. The others cheered him on with words of encouragement. Then all they could do was wait.

'HOOFIUS WAS NOT A WINNER,' cackled the voice from below. 'TREVOR—COME ON DOWN!'

'Huh? Where's Hoofius?' asked the mushroom. Hoofius had gone in but not come out, just like Bingo had said. 'This is bad,' Trevor said, his lip wobbling.

'Sure is,' said the genie. 'I don't have enough pennies for parking. I'll have to fly the carpet around until you're finished.'

The four friends were more worried about the fate of the faun. Trevor took his turn, and again the minutes passed. The not knowing was the worst of all. What was going on down there?

'Let's play a game,' said Blossom, trying to take their minds off it. 'I spy with my unicorn eye something . . .' He looked around the empty desert. '. . . Beginning with CC!'

'It's Creepy Crypt, isn't it?' said Twinkle.

'How did you know?' asked the unicorn, just as the voice called out again.

Herbert waited as Blossom and then Twinkle took their turns and didn't come out.

Herbert's turn came at last. The walls guided him down through the gloom, and he found himself in a pitch-black room. There was no sign of the others. A dazzling flame lit up the chamber to reveal a large wheel on the wall. But that wasn't all. There was a face within the fire.

It's time to play . . .
WHEEL OF MISFORTUNE!
With me—your host—
FLAMING SKULL FACE!

'Welcome, contestant! What's your name and where do you come from?' cackled the host.

'What's going on? Where are my friends?' demanded Herbert.

'Eh-ehhh! Wrong answer!' laughed the skull. Herbert realized he'd have to play along to have any hope of getting out or seeing his friends again. He listened carefully as Flaming Skull Face explained the rules of the trial.

'You spin the wheel. If you land on the trial gem, you WIN! If you land on a skull, you DIE! I mean—you LOSE! And if you land on a question, then you have to answer it correctly to stay in the game and spin again! NOW . . . LET'S SPIN THAT WHEEL!'

The first spin landed on a question, and a flame lit up five coffins standing upright along the wall.
1
2

3
4
5

'Use the following clues to correctly identify the empty coffin,' said the host. 'And don't forget to play along at home!'

Herbert wasn't quite sure what that last part meant, but he studied the coffins carefully as the clues were read out.

'The empty coffin has one sad face and more than one rubber duck. It has fewer than two eyes, and an odd number of skeletons.'

Herbert's eyes darted across the coffins as the clues played back in his mind. Was it one or more rubber ducks? And what number of skeletons?

I'm going to have to push you for an answer!

'Number four!' Herbert said at last.

'Let's open that coffin!' shrieked the host. The door swung open, and to Herbert's relief, the coffin was empty. He was still in the game. He spun the wheel again, and this time it landed on a happy face.

'You've won a PRIZE! That's right, you and a friend are off on an all-expenses-paid trip to a luxury elven spa!' said the skull, before adding, 'or . . . you can swap it all for the MYSTERY PRIZE!'

A box hovered in front of Herbert. Not being one for massages and smelly elven oils, he decided to open it.

The wheel spun once more. For a heart-stopping moment, it looked like it was landing on the skull tile.

'Another question round!' said Flaming Skull Face. 'We gave one hundred doomed adventurers one hundred seconds to name something they wish they had taken with them into the desert. You need to give us the TOP THREE answers. You can confer with a friend . . . if you had one, that is! AHA HA!'

Herbert racked his brains. If he was a doomed adventurer, what would he need? Then it struck him: maybe he WAS a doomed adventurer.

'Let's have some answers!' shrieked the skull, its fire blazing even more, as if sensing the dramatic conclusion to the game or trial or whatever this was.

'Water!' said Herbert. 'And . . . a map?'

'Ding! Ding! CORRECT!' spat the skull.

Herbert needed one more, but his mind was coming up blank. Flaming Skull Face whizzed around the chamber, sparks fizzing out as it went.

'Maybe . . . a weapon of some sort? Or a picnic?' Herbert muttered to himself.

'Tick-tock!' cackled the skull.

'SUN CREAM!' came the response. 'THE DOOMED ADVENTURERS WOULD HAVE WANTED SUN CREAM IN THE DESERT!'

A chilling laugh echoed around the chamber.

Is that your final answer?

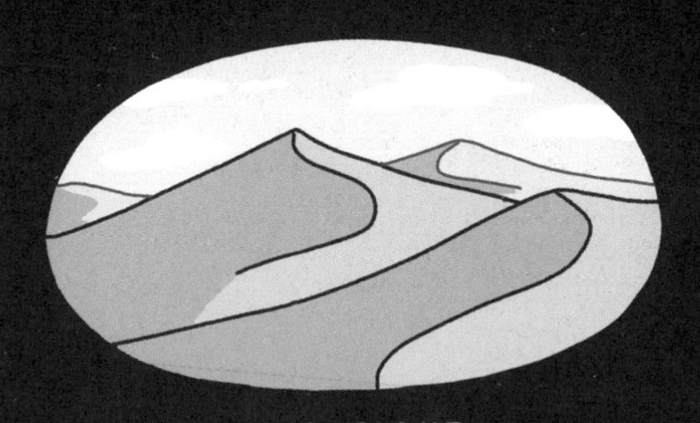

CHAPTER EIGHT

TRIAL AND TERROR

The truth was, it wasn't Herbert's final answer at all. The voice wasn't his. It came from within the puzzle cube.

'Ding! CORRECT!' said the skull. 'It's time to SPIN THAT WHEEL!'

Herbert breathed a deep sigh of relief.

'Thank you, Tiddlywink,' he said before giving the wheel another spin. He stood back and watched as it clattered to a halt on the trial gem. Herbert had won.

'Congratulations, Herbert! You leave today with a weekend break at the Ogre Swamp and the star prize: a trial gem! How do you feel?' asked the skull, its flames beginning to burn out.

'I'll feel just fine when I see that my friends are unharmed!' said the gnome.

The skull gave one last cackle and fell to the floor, the flames extinguished. The trial gem rolled out of its mouth.

Herbert grabbed the gem as torches in the chamber flickered into life. The doors of the four closed coffins opened, and out fell his friends in a heap on the ground.

They trudged up and out into the sunlight, swapping stories of the chamber. Hoofius and Twinkle had landed on the skull straight away—an instant loss. Trevor failed a round where he had to guess the price of ancient relics, and Blossom had answered 'bubblegum' as something a doomed adventurer would have wanted in the desert.

'Thankfully I had the sharp ears and mind of Tiddlywink to help me out of a pickle,' said Herbert, giving the pixie his due. Not that he needed it.

'YOU'D ALL BE FOOD FOR WORMS IN THOSE COFFINS IF IT WASN'T FOR ME,' said the pixie cheerily. 'I TRUST YOU'LL REMEMBER

THIS AT THE BALLOT BOX WHEN I RUN FOR RE-ELECTION TO THE COUNCIL OF HAPPINESS!'

How Tiddlywink kept getting voted on to the council seemed like one of the many mysteries of the Super Happy Magic Forest. There were none so prickly and short-tempered as the pixie. But you couldn't deny that his no-nonsense approach played well with the public. Even if he never made it out, you could bet toffee pennies on people voting for an angry cube.

'*THE MANY TRIALS OF TIDDLYWINK*,' mused the pixie. 'THAT'LL BE A FITTING NAME FOR THE BOOK THEY'LL WRITE ABOUT MY EPIC QUEST.'

'Sounds like a bestseller,' said Trevor, struggling to keep a straight face.

'I would read it!' said Blossom, to everyone's surprise.

'I thought you liked comics and books with lots of pictures,' said Hoofius. Why Blossom would be interested in Tiddlywink's vanity project he had no idea.

'THERE WILL BE PICTURES! LOTS OF THEM!' barked the pixie. 'I'M GOOD AT PICTURES. MAMA ALWAYS PUT MY DRAWINGS ON THE FRIDGE WHEN I WAS JUST A KIDDLYWINK.'

'See?' said Blossom. 'Tiddlywink is a great artist!'

Blossom felt he had to be extra nice to Tiddlywink, given the situation he had landed him in. And he felt more than a bit bad about his own performance in the last trial.

'Hey, where's Bingo?' asked Twinkle. 'And the carpet? They're not here!'

They scanned the empty skies.

'I KNEW THAT GENIE WAS NOT TO BE TRUSTED!' said the pixie. 'SHE HAS STOLEN THE MAGIC CARPET AND LEFT US ALL FOR DEAD!'

'Why would I need a magic carpet?' said Bingo, popping out from seemingly nowhere. 'I can already fly. I'm a glorified cloud, remember?'

That shut up Tiddlywink.

'I knew Bingo and the carpet would still be here,' said Blossom.

'Actually, the carpet is gone,' said Bingo. 'It shook me off and away it went. They don't stay tame for long. They yearn to fly wild and free. Or lie in a hallway.'

They had no choice but to trek through the sand towards the last trial.

'Bingo, where are we going for the last gem?' asked Hoofius.

'I thought you'd never ask!' said the genie. 'Follow me.'

It seemed to the heroes that Bingo was leading them nowhere. For all the walking they were doing, the landscape wasn't changing.

I spy with my unicorn eye . . .
Sand dunes. It can only be sand dunes.

'Bingo, we've been walking for ages,' complained Twinkle. 'Can't you find the trial?'

'It's more a case of the trial finding us,' said the genie. 'And even then, the trial itself could be anything. The host's mind and mood can shift like the sands.'

The heroes were in no mood for mystery. They dived into the first spot of shade they found.

'What's wrong with all of you?' asked Bingo, trying to prod them back into action. 'You're not dying, are you? Mortals are always doing that.'

Herbert removed a boot and tipped it upside down. As the sand poured out, the whole dune began to shift beneath them and seemed to be morphing to a gigantic size.

'I didn't think I had this much sand in my boot,' said Herbert while it grew and grew.

Bingo didn't seem concerned. 'Here we go!' she said. 'This is the last trial. Everybody, say hello to the spirit of the desert . . .

. . . the Sandyman!'

'WHAT'S GOING ON OUT THERE?' cried Tiddlywink. He was none the wiser that a huge sand monster was looming over them.

There was no response from the heroes. They had been caught up in an avalanche that threatened to bury them and their hopes of making it out of the desert alive. They struggled against the tide, desperate not to become separated and lost beneath the dunes.

'Sandyman, stop!' yelled Bingo, realizing her new friends were in a pickle.

But the sands continued to fall.

CHAPTER NINE

THE ACE OF SPADES

Bingo had been hovering above the rush of sand that engulfed the heroes, and it took some sharp reactions from the genie to dive down and pluck them out like carrots from the dirt before they disappeared.

'Sorry,' rumbled the Sandyman. Realizing the trouble he'd caused by his grand entrance, he morphed into a much more agreeable size.

Is this better for you?
You could have started at that size.

Bingo introduced her new friends and told the Sandyman about their quest for trial gems. The two seemed to be on familiar terms, which made sense given Bingo had wandered the desert for a thousand years.

'Then all that stands between you and the Oracle is my trial,' said the Sandyman. 'I hope you're prepared for the . . . ULTIMATE CHALLENGE!'

As it happened, the heroes didn't feel very prepared at all. Herbert hadn't even got his boot back on. But it was all that stood between them and freeing Tiddlywink.

The Sandyman disappeared within the dunes and surged back to the surface with tools they'd need to take part in the trial.

The heroes couldn't quite believe their eyes.

You're building sandcastles. Please use the buckets and spades provided.

'You must sculpt a perfect sandcastle using this cool, compact sand from the desert floor,' explained the Sandyman. 'I'll be waiting.'

He collapsed back into a billion grains, leaving the heroes alone in the baking heat of the desert.

'Wait, that's it?' asked Hoofius. 'No roaring crowd? Or showbiz presenter?'

'Yup,' said Bingo. 'With the Sandyman, what you see is what you get. Sand.'

The heroes picked up their tools and got to work.

But crafting a perfect sandcastle was easier said than done.

A little flag on top would have been nice.
What happened here?
Buckets and spades are hard.

By now Bingo was starting to panic. 'What's wrong?' she asked the heroes. 'Sandcastles are mega easy! Look!'

Her arms became a mad blur of movement before she revealed a superb-looking castle. It even had a working drawbridge.

'We don't have a thousand years of practice,' said Trevor, unimpressed.

'Or any little flags,' said Twinkle.

The heroes began to sweat, and not just from the sun. They had only one shot at the trial gem left.

And its name was Blossom.

The Sandyman and the heroes moved on to the final competitor.

The desert spirit made happy rumbling sounds while watching Blossom work. For all the secret troubles the unicorn carried with him in the desert, Blossom had managed to lose himself in the joy of carefree creation.

'Yes, yes!' said the Sandyman. 'This is it! This is what I was waiting for!'

'It . . . is?' said Bingo, flabbergasted. To the questing adventurers, Blossom's sandcastle looked like it had already been kicked over, with a couple of stomps thrown in for good measure.

'The perfect sandcastle is crafted by the heart, not the head,' said the Sandyman.

Blossom had barely even noticed they were there, such was the fun he was having.

'Oh, Twinkle! Can I borrow your wand?' he asked. Twinkle handed it over, and Blossom rammed it into what the others assumed must be the top of the castle.

'Ahhh, a castle sculpted with pure love and joy,' said the Sandyman. 'There's not a grain out of place.'

'Does the Sandyman have eyes?' whispered Trevor to the others.

'Ssssh!' said Bingo, giving him a nudge.

The desert spirit dived into the dunes and a hand burst out, offering up a trial gem.

'I know it's a little earlier than usual,' said Hoofius, 'but we do have all the trial gems. I feel it's time for a . . .'

The heroes said their farewells to the Sandyman, but not before he had given them a handy ride to the edge of the Sea of Sand.

With all three trial gems, they set their sights on the Almighty Oracle. This time, things would be different.

CHAPTER TEN

CRYSTAL UNCLEAR

Soon they were once again headed towards the rocky peak upon which the Almighty Oracle floated. Only this time, they were ready. They had endured the toughest tests the desert had to offer and passed with flying colours (and even a flying carpet, at one point).

'You did it, mortals!' cheered Bingo. 'I have to admit, I wasn't sure you could take the heat. But you've conquered the Desert Trials! There is something special about you five.'

Blossom was beaming from the sandcastle trial. He'd won them the final trial gem, and he'd even had fun doing it! Tiddlywink would be freed soon. *And I reckon he'll be so happy about it that he'll forget all about finding who was to blame for putting him in the box*, thought the unicorn.

'Great news, Tiddlywink!' said Herbert. 'You'll be out in no time.'

There was no answer from the cube.

'Maybe he's fallen asleep,' offered Hoofius, as a concerned Herbert took the box out of his bag. Come to think of it, Tiddlywink had been quiet for the whole trek and trial in the Sea of Sand, and, usually, you couldn't sneeze without the pixie having something to say about it.

'Tiddlywink?' said Herbert, panic in his voice.

'HELLO? CAN ANYONE HEAR ME?' came the voice from inside.

'Tiddlywink sounds different,' said Twinkle. 'It's like he's very far away.'

'Uh-oh,' said Bingo. 'It's one of *those* puzzle boxes. Back when these things were all the rage, a second edition was made that slowly sucked the life out of whoever was inside until they faded away completely. The boxes were banned soon after. Turned out they were a bit of a choking hazard.'

'Then we don't have much time!' yelled Blossom. He grabbed the cube out of Herbert's hands and began hotfooting it towards the peak.

'I'm not sure he's ever moved so fast,' gasped Twinkle, as the others raced to keep up. They assembled at the top, with the resting face of the Oracle floating before them. Herbert slotted each trial gem into place, and the gems began to glow. Then the Oracle opened its eyes.

THE ORACLE FINDS YOU WORTHY. A QUESTION EACH IS BESTOWED UPON YOU. ASK ME ANYTHING.
INSERT TRUST GEMS HERE

'How do we solve this puzzle?' Blossom asked, holding up the cube to meet the empty gaze of the big crystal face.

'EASY,' spoke the Oracle. **'FOLLOW MY INSTRUCTIONS.'**

Blossom listened and began to twist the box.

'NEXT QUESTION,' boomed the Oracle. It gave the impression that it was in a hurry to get back to doing nothing.

'Where is my lamp?' blurted Bingo, who could hardly contain herself.

'EASY. THE LAMP LIES WITHIN THE FORGOTTEN TEMPLE.'

'Ooh! I forgot about that temple!' squealed Bingo, doing a loop-the-loop of excitement.

By now Blossom had finished twisting the cube. But nothing happened. He turned it over in his hands. Two symbols were in the wrong place!

'But I followed it exactly!' he said aloud, as they all stared at the uncompleted puzzle.

'We can ask again,' said Hoofius. 'We still have questions left. Let me try.'

The Oracle gave instructions again, and everyone watched as Hoofius carefully followed along. There was to be no mistake this time. At least, not from Hoofius.

But the puzzle was still unsolved.

The Oracle tried again. And again. But it still couldn't crack the cube.

'Hey!' yelled Blossom to the floating face. 'We're following it all precisely, but YOU are getting it wrong. Aren't you supposed to know EVERYTHING?'

The face began to shudder and blip as it attempted to answer for a final time.

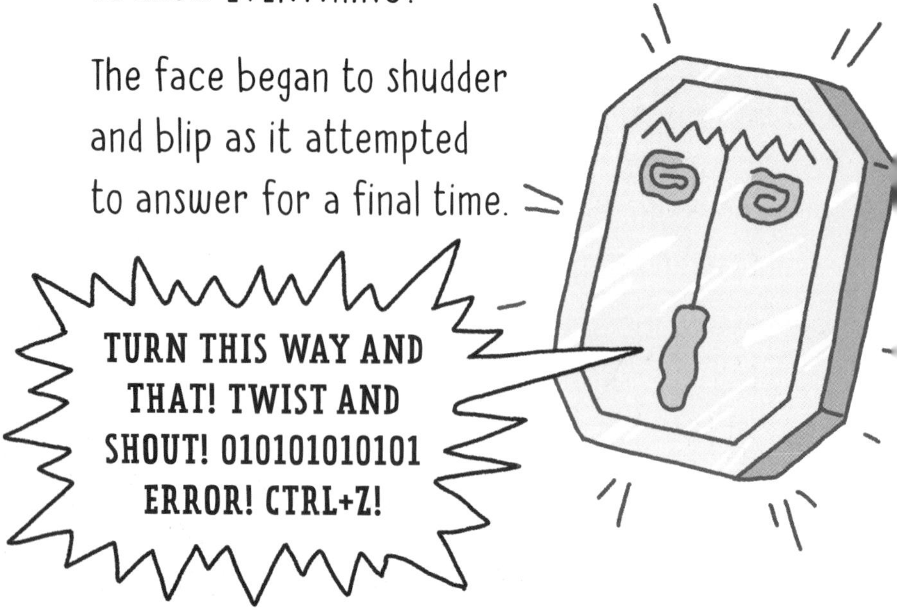

TURN THIS WAY AND THAT! TWIST AND SHOUT! 010101010101 ERROR! CTRL+Z!

Its eyes flickered, and its cool clear sheen started glowing red. The heroes took a few steps back.

Something had gone horribly wrong.

'MALFUNCTION DETECTED. ANSWER COMMAND NOT RECOGNIZED. MUST DESTROY ALL WITNESSES TO PRESERVE REPUTATION.'

'Great. We've broken the Almighty Oracle,' said Trevor. 'Nothing is ever built to last these days.'

'We have to leave!' cried Bingo.

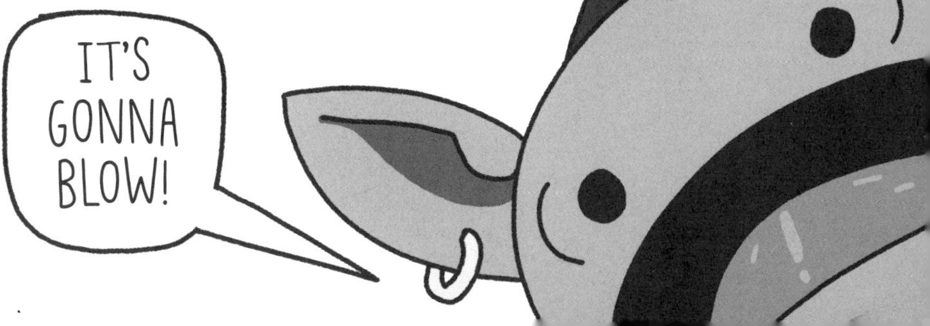

IT'S
GONNA
BLOW!

DESTRUCTION MODE ACTIVATED!
Maybe we forgot to say please and thank you.
This is the worst tourist attraction ever.

It's still more fun than the Wizard City Library.
WHAT'S GOING ON? ARE THOSE GOOD NOISES?

They scrambled away from the Oracle and down the rocky peak to safety, leaving the face in a confused rampage high above.

'Will it follow us?' asked Hoofius, trying to get his breath back.

'That thing has done nothing but float there for thousands of years,' said Bingo. 'And it just fired lasers out its eyes. So I'd say anything is possible.'

The only noise now was the faintest sound of sniffing and blubbing from a pixie doomed to fade away into oblivion.

The sands of time had run out.

CHAPTER ELEVEN
THE UNICORN DID IT

'I . . . CAN'T HOLD ON MUCH LONGER,' whimpered Tiddlywink. 'I TRIED TO BE A GOOD PIXIE . . .' His voice sounded further away than ever. '. . . I ALWAYS DID WHAT I THOUGHT WAS BEST FOR THE SUPER HAPPY MAGIC FOREST . . .'

The heroes exchanged glances, but nobody said anything. They couldn't deny Tiddlywink his final words, however fanciful they might seem.

'. . . TELL ADMIN BUNNY . . . I STILL WANT THAT REPORT ON MY DESK BY FRIDAY,' continued the pixie. 'AND . . . SUNSHINE . . . TELL SUNSHINE I NEVER LIKED HIS JOKES . . . AND . . . BUTTERFLY HORSE THAT . . . I KNOW IT WAS HER . . . WHO . . . TRAMPLED MY FLOWERS THAT ONE TIME . . .'

'I'm so sorry, Tiddlywink. I never should have put on that exhibition,' sobbed Herbert, dabbing his eyes with a hanky. 'I'm a silly old fool.'

Now, now. You're not *that* old.

Blossom had heard enough. *This isn't fair,* he thought. *Herbert shouldn't have to take the blame for what I did. I have to come clean.* He took a deep breath.

'I'm the fool,' said Blossom, his lip wobbling. 'I played with the puzzle box. I'm sorry . . . I didn't know it would trap Tiddlywink!'

Tears rolled down Blossom's cheeks and fizzed away into the sand. He felt an arm on his shoulder.

It was Bingo.

'Quit it with the waterworks! We've all made mistakes,' said the genie. 'Believe me, I've made some *bad* ones. But it seems to me that everything you've done since making yours has been to try to put it right.'

'But I should have been honest about what happened!' continued Blossom. 'I should have told everyone straight away. I was scared of what they'd all say. I didn't want to be evicted from the forest! I understand if you never want to see or speak to me again,' he said to the others. 'I'll stay here in the desert. It might not be so bad.'

'You're right, Blossom. You *should* have told us,' said Herbert. 'You made a mistake by fiddling with the cube. And then not telling us what you did was an even bigger mistake! I nearly took the blame for you! But we would have understood and moved forward together. That's what friends do.'

'I agree,' said Hoofius. 'And we all know you'd not survive long in the desert without candyfloss and hot chocolate before bedtime. We aren't leaving you here.'

You guys are the best.
Well, obviously!
I KNEW IT! YOU'RE ALL IN IT TOGETHER!

The heroes jumped in surprise at the sudden eruption from the cube.

'I'M ABOUT TO DISAPPEAR ENTIRELY, AND YOU LOT ARE HIGH-FIVING EACH OTHER FOR TALKING ABOUT YOUR FEELINGS! THIS WAS PROBABLY ALL PART OF YOUR GRAND PLAN TO GET ME OFF THE COUNCIL. WHO PUT YOU UP TO IT? WAS IT SUNSHINE?'

Clearly, Blossom's admission had got Tiddlywink's blood racing and brought the pixie back from the brink.

'There's life in him yet,' said Trevor.

'Then we still have a chance!' said Bingo. 'Before it went doolally, the Oracle told me where my lamp was. If we find it, you can wish him out of there!'

'We haven't failed a quest yet,' said Hoofius. 'Let's get that lamp!'

'Where was it? I can't remember,' said Blossom.

'The Forgotten Temple,' said Bingo excitedly. 'It's hidden among the cliffs in the north-eastern reaches of the desert. I never thought of looking in there. Let's go!'

By now the heroes were used to the aches and pains and discomfort of desert questing. But they still couldn't wait to leave it far behind.

'When we get home, I'm jumping into Lake Sparkle and never coming out,' said Twinkle, as they hurried towards their destination.

Sure enough, the Forgotten Temple was right where Bingo said it would be.

Musty air greeted them as they stepped inside. Cobwebs covered every crevice and corner of the narrow passages. It was so quiet that they would almost have welcomed the cackle of a burning skull.

'This place must be really old,' observed Blossom. 'Older than that cheese Herbert puts on his crackers.'

'Be careful where you tread and what you touch,' said Bingo, leading the way. 'These ancient temples are prime places for booby traps.'

But no sooner had the genie finished speaking than a shriek tore through the corridors behind them and sent a chill down their spines.

The heroes spun on their heels and hooves.

The sound was like nothing they'd ever heard before.

'It was terrifying!' said Twinkle.

'It was horrifying!' said Herbert.

It was Hoofius.
EEEE! Get away!
But I live here.

'Hoofius, get a grip!' grumbled Twinkle as the spider skittered through a crack in the wall.

'My lampy senses are tingling!' squealed Bingo. She seemed to know which way to go, drawn to her lamp like a moth to a flame. But she didn't see the secret scythe trap lying in wait.

Being able to disarm any traps as they went was certainly another handy feature of Bingo. If this had been a desert trial for mortals only, things might have been messy.

A few faint words leaked out from the puzzle box, reminding them of the minutes or even seconds they had remaining.

'Come on! We're nearly there,' said Bingo, hardly able to contain her excitement.

The corridors twisted and turned, and deeper into the temple they went.

And then they found it.

CHAPTER TWELVE

LET'S GET READY TO CRUMBLE

While most folks travelled the Distant Desert looking for water, only the sight of her lamp again could quench Bingo's thirst. She had often wondered if the moment would ever come when she would see it again after it was hidden away all those years ago.

And now it was happening so fast.

MY LAMP!
Looks like a teapot!
Big Face was right about something.

PANTHIA
Bingo

'Hold up! Everybody stay still!' called Bingo, fearing another trap. The sight of her lamp just sitting there felt too good to be true. But for Blossom, the urge to run and grab it and wish away everything was too strong to resist. Not for the first time, he ignored the warnings.

A loud click sounded as he lifted the lamp off the pedestal.

'What was that noise?' asked Twinkle.

The whole chamber began to shake and rumble. Chunks of rock came loose and fell around them.

'It's a BOOBY TRAP!' yelled Bingo.

The heroes struggled to stay on their feet as everything shook. Blossom took a tumble, and the lamp clattered away. A violent crack ripped the floor open, and they watched the lamp fall through the gap.

Blossom leapt towards the chasm but felt an arm pull him back.

'Leave it!' said Bingo. 'We have to get out of here or you'll all be squished flat!'

'What about Tiddlywink?' cried Blossom.

'Not all mistakes can be undone,' said Bingo. 'I learned that the hard way. But not getting you five out of here alive would be my biggest mistake ever!'

There was a crunching sound as a huge slab dislodged from the ceiling and looked set to flatten the heroes. Bingo let go of Blossom and shot up to meet it.

Go! I'll be okay. Made of magic, remember?

'Blossom, come on!' shouted Twinkle from the doorway. 'This whole place is going to crumble into dust!'

'We did our best,' cried Herbert. 'Please, Blossom!' He and the others were at the edge of the chamber, desperate for the unicorn to join them.

But Blossom had always been one for ignoring good advice. He turned away from his friends and scrambled over to the jagged hole in the floor. He could see Bingo's lamp perched above a dark abyss.

It was just out of reach.

Bingo was straining under the weight of the fallen ceiling. 'I can't . . . hold it much longer!' she called as Blossom stretched towards the lamp.

The chamber shook again, and Blossom fell in.

He felt himself rushing towards the darkness.

But it never came.

Herbert's hand was wrapped around Blossom's leg. Blossom hooked the lamp handle on his horn as his friends hauled him up and out of the abyss. They hurried towards the doorway and away from Bingo.

'Lift the lid on the lamp!' called the genie, sinking lower and lower towards the floor under the enormous weight. 'And stand back!'

Blossom did as he was told. Bingo was sucked into the lamp like water down a plughole. The huge slab dropped to the floor and smashed from the impact.

Blossom rubbed, and Bingo burst out.

'Quickly! Do a wish!' cried Bingo.

Rocks, debris, and dust were falling like rain on them now. Pretty soon the Forgotten Temple would be a forgotten pile of rubble.

'Okay, here goes,' cried Blossom. 'I wish we were all safely back outside!'

Bingo felt the fizz and pop of genie magic through her veins once again.

This time, it was all for real.

CHAPTER THIRTEEN

ONE LAST WISH

In a flash, the cacophony and chaos of the crumbling temple cut to the quiet stillness of a familiar desert oasis. It took a few dizzy seconds before they realized where they were and what had happened.

Quite sure he said SAFELY outside.
Whoops. Still a bit rusty.

'It worked!' cheered Blossom. 'You're all okay!' The heroes looked groggy, with the odd new cut and bruise to add to their desert collection, but they were in one piece.

'Blossom, the cube!' choked Herbert. The poor gnome had inhaled quite a bit of dust.

'Bingo, I wish for Tiddlywink to be released from the cube!' cried Blossom.

The heroes hoped with all their hearts that they weren't too late.

Bingo got to work, the cube rising into the air and spinning around, each picture turning and clicking into place. The cube fell to the floor, the puzzle finally complete. It rocked back and forth a couple of times, and the heroes held their breath.

And then out came the pixie.

The heroes watched as Tiddlywink writhed around in the sand. They had never been so happy to see him. Or indeed, happy to see him at all. But he was here and that was all that mattered.

'Nice to finally meet you, Tiddlywink,' said Bingo. 'Your friends were just telling me that the Super-Duper Happy Forest would fall apart if you weren't there keeping things in order.' She gave Blossom a wink.

'They said that?' murmured Tiddlywink, who snapped out of his writhing and dusted himself down.

'Well, of course!' Tiddlywink stood up straight and puffed out his chest.

First things first: a second opening ceremony for the new rainbow slide.

'He's back,' observed Trevor. 'In body *and* soul.'

'Then we completed the quest!' cheered Hoofius. 'The Super Happy Heroes have done it again!'

'Thank you all so much for helping to reunite me with my long-lost lamp,' said Bingo. 'You may be mortals, but I'll remember you for as long as I live. Or at least for the first few hundred years or so. After that, who knows.'

'We'll take it!' laughed Herbert, who was as relieved as anyone that Tiddlywink had escaped safely from the puzzle box.

'So, what'll wish number three be?' asked Bingo.

'I suppose I should wish for us all to be back in the forest,' said Blossom. It wasn't a fun way to spend a last wish, but it felt like the right thing to do. The journey back home would be a long one, and Tiddlywink was already feeling the heat.

'Wait!' said Herbert, as Blossom geared up to make the wish. 'Look!'

Across the water, a familiar magic carpet lay stretched out on the sand.

Twinkle was already sneaking up to it.

Trevor turned to Tiddlywink. 'Get ready for the ride of your life.'

They skimmed across the skies, enjoying the cooler air against their faces.

In the far distance, they spied the Almighty Oracle blasting the sand with its laser eyes.

'Umm . . . should we do something about that?' asked Hoofius.

'Nah. I'm sure it'll wear itself out,' shrugged Bingo. She saw Blossom staring down at her lamp, pondering his last wish. 'Make it a fun one,' she whispered to him. 'You deserve it.'

The carpet carried them all the way home to the Super Happy Magic Forest. The reception for the heroes flying in the skies above was raucous, to say the least . . .

I'm back, everyone! Never fear! I had it all under control. Hoo-ho!
Wow! Enchanted rug!
They did it! They . . . what were they doing?
I don't know. Just smile and wave.

Tiddlywink is back!
Suppose I'll clear my things out of his office.

'My travels in the desert were long and tough,' declared Tiddlywink, signalling for everyone to be quiet. '. . . And I am delighted to announce that public funds *will be secured* to publish a full chronicle of my quest!'

There was a slight ripple of applause and more than the odd grumble.

'*His* quest?' said Bingo to the others.

'It'll be a pretty short book,' said Trevor.

'I'll look forward to the bit about when he got the sniffles,' added Twinkle.

'Hey!' said the pixie, turning away from his public. 'Those tears were down to an allergic reaction I had in the desert and nothing more!'

He turned back to the crowd. 'And now to more grave matters. I am sorry to announce the reason for my disappearance. These five you call *the heroes* are perhaps not so heroic at all! Indeed, it was actually Blossom who–'

Before Tiddlywink could finish, Blossom stood up and held the lamp above his head. 'I WISH FOR TEN THOUSAND ICE CREAMS!' he screamed. Ice cream rained from the skies, and Tiddlywink's accusations were drowned out by the cheers of delirious forest folk.

With the quest complete, there was only one thing left to do . . .

. . . EAT!
Wow! What a scoop!
PRESS

BLOSSOM! BLOSSOM! BLOSSOM!
Well, that's me out of business.
URGH!
Another quest in the books. Surely the heroes deserve some time off!
You know, I think you might be right.

With the drama of the desert quest behind him, Blossom vowed to never fiddle with forbidden things again.
So this is where Herbert hides his honey . . .
DANGER! BEES
DO NOT APPROACH
It didn't last.
AHHHHHHHHH!
Herbert never went on his free trip to the Ogre Swamp . . .

I don't think he's coming.
I made this mud and bone pie for nothing!
WELCOME PRIZE WINNER

. . . but he did enjoy having the magic carpet lie in his hallway. Until it all went wrong.

Bingo eventually returned to the Distant Desert, ready to relax with her lamp and with all loose ends tied up . . .

And the Sandyman agreed to bury the cursed puzzle cube so deep that nobody would ever find it.

Because some things are better left alone.

MATTY LONG

Game show host? AHAHAHAHA! Don't quit your day job!

As a young boy Matty always thought he would grow up to be a game show host. But instead he became the next best thing: an illustrator and author! He has mostly made picture books, and this is his first chapter book series so he hopes you like it and want to tell everyone.

After wanting a cat and instead buying fish, Matty now has a sausage dog called Sherman. But he still wants a cat.

You can find him online at www.mattylong.com.

ALSO BY MATTY LONG

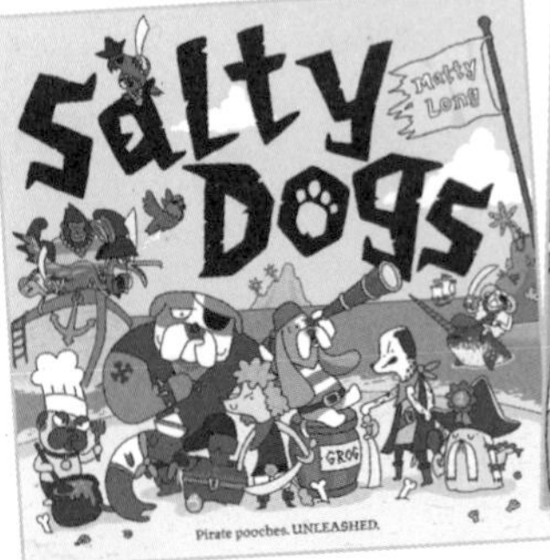